ELEMENT

A Lindsay Leahy, David Leahy story

Pharos Books

ISBN: 978-93-5546-111-7
eISBN: 978-93-5546-112-4

©**Author**

Publisher: Pharos Books (P) Ltd.
Plot No.-55, Main Mother Dairy Road
Pandav Nagar, East Delhi-110092
Phone: 011-40395855, +14049995474
WhatsApp: +91 8368220032
E-mail: sales@pharosbooks.in
Website: www.pharosbooks.in
First Edition: 2022

Printed By: Sushma Book Binding House, Okhla
Industrial Area, Phase II, New Delhi-110020

ELEMENT
A Lindsay Leahy, David Leahy story

CONTENTS

BOOK-1 : ELEMENT

BOOK-2 : ELECTRA

PROLOGUE

My name is Emily Kat Jones and I am 'Element'. This is my story; about me and all the hardships, I went through as a kid to an adult. My mom, was a drug addict, with whom I lived up to the age of 5 after which I went into foster care. I got adopted by a nice old man by the name of Jamie but he died 5 years later when I was 10. Upon his death, I was adopted by a team named Power Girls. I think they felt sorry for me and adopted me. Anyway, I know it's a stupid name they have, right? But they are good people.

Years later I left them to join the army when I was 18. Through the army, I met my best friends Rachel and Eli. I was a part of a Black Ops team in the year 2040. I will talk about them as I continue the story.

Chapter 1

As I left the Power Girls when I was 18 to join the army, I subsequently joined the Black Ops team.

It was made of 2 people — myself and our captain, who is also the father of one of the best friends I was going to have. My Captain's name is Jamie St. Peter's and my best friends are Rachel Charlotte and Eli St. Peter's. I met them during the war. Eli and I got an order to check on a secret chemical weapon but while testing it blew up, causing radiation, with a green substance splashing all over. It splattered on both of us well. Yes, it was a little foolish of us to have stayed there, we should have run away, but I wouldn't be Element without it and Eli wouldn't be Briner. The enormous blow had knocked us out and when we woke up we had powers— extraordinary powers. When Rachel saw us she thought that we were dead but we were not, we just got our powers. Rachel thought that she saw a ghost. But she was seeing what she had hoped for. She had hoped that we were alive, and we were alive. But we didn't want to see her like this— as what we had become. She would give up hope of us being alive or dead when she would look at us, so we disappeared like we were ghosts. But she missed us; we were her best friends. Soon after we saw Rachel, Eli told me that he liked me but I didn't like him back, which caused him to freak out. He ended up using his powers on me to hypnotize me to fall in love with him just like he wanted.

Chapter 2

After the war, we met St Peter's, Eli's father. As he looked at us, he thanked God that we were alive. He asked us what had happened that day and to us. We told him everything and showed him our powers. He was shocked and couldn't believe a thing we said. Right after our funeral he dropped his mouth open and asked if Rachel knows that we were alive. We told him that she does not have any idea that we are alive and we are going to stay away from her, at least for now, until we learn to control our powers.

Chapter 3

The next morning, while we were at St. Peters', I got up, and soon after Eli did too. We wished St. Peter's a good morning and he wished us right back. The T.V. in his living room was on and a news channel was playing. The news said something about an ancient ruin. I turned up the volume and we listened to it carefully. It said that it might be an alien ruin that was left there for someone to find at last. I was intrigued and suggested that we should go to the ruin and check it out. Eli thought this was a crazy idea. He said that it could really hurt us or worse we could die from it.

"Why do you want to go there anyway?" Eli said.

"I need to go, I must go there. It's just a feeling that I have to. And we have our powers so what can go wrong?" I insisted.

Jamie agreed with me and said "why not? we sure can go."

I was so excited, but Eli did not want to go. He thought it was a bad idea. But the look on my face was so cute that he had to say yes. Later that night, we all went to the ruin. We found an alien ship. There was something inscribed on the ship— in an unusual language, but I could read it. It said *I am Element hear me sing*. Reading that, I thought I should perhaps sing. As I did, it opened. I found it confusing and weird that it opened for me. I moved towards the ship but Eli stopped me.

"What are you doing?" He exclaimed.

I told him that I'm going inside the ship. Yet again, he thought it was a crazy idea even for us who have powers.

"Look Eli I'll be fine" I tried to reassure him.

Jaime backed me.

"But dad Emily doesn't know what is in there, it could be dangerous in there," Eli was persistent.

"Look, son, don't worry, she will be fine. You worry too much" Jamie said.

"Okay, I will let her but I'm going with her!" said Eli.

We quickly moved and went inside the ship with Jaime waiting for us outside. We went in not knowing what to expect but we saw an old costume, a super-suit perhaps, just hanging there that had not been worn in years.

"Umm... Emily?"

"What, Eli?"

Eli thought to himself if he should tell me how he feels about me. He was worried that if his powers didn't work on me, I might reject him. He thought to himself "would we be friends and only that?"

Scared and worried he wanted to kiss me. He leaned down to kiss me and he did it. It was a passionate kiss. We were almost on each other. But Eli stopped, he said that we shouldn't go farther than this because we are friends. In that hurried passionate moment, we had hit something and a hologram popped up. It said:

"If you are watching this I'm dead, Emily. I'm your father and my name is Craig Jones. You're my daughter and I love you. I'm so sorry I left you and your mother but I had to go back to my planet. I am from the planet Element."

"Wait ... What... This can't be...I'm confused" was my only reaction to what I was hearing.

The hologram continued "I know you have powers now, Emily. Take the power gloves. They will help you control your new powers just like they helped me when I was alive."

I took the gloves. They were like half gloves. They were pink to match the super suit, which had a white top, with a pink lower and a pink cape. I tried it on. It fit me as if it was meant for me, which of course I thought was a little creepy but cool at the same time. Eli said that I look wonderful in it and I replied with thanks and kissed him on the cheek.

He blushed and asked, "why did you do it?"

I said, "because I love you."

But Eli thought to himself, "does she mean just as a friend? What if she means more than that? Maybe if I just ask her about that..."

So he did ask me about it and I said "of course more, duh! And as a friend at the same time."

We came out of the ship like nothing was wrong. Jamie asked if anything had happened.

I said, "not really but I'm half alien and I found out where my father comes from. I got a cool super suit as well."

Eli however thought to himself that it was so stupid of me to say that. "She didn't say that she was in love with me, maybe she doesn't want dad to worry about us and where we are going from here."

They got out of the ruin and took a flight back home.

Chapter 4

As Rachel was trekking in the mountains, she went to the west side of the mountains and found an old temple there. Master Leo Lee was inside. He was the master of the temple. "I am Rachel Charlotte, it's lovely to meet you. I want to be your student."

He said, "I'm Leo Lee and if you want to become my student, you have to pass 3 tests."

"I will pass your tests," she was affirmative.

Soon after, her tests began. Her first task was to run up a huge flight of stairs, which was followed by her second test which was to balance herself at 100 feet height. Her final test was to make him a perfect green tea. She passed all the tests and it was agreed that master Lee will train her. Her training began and she learned to use the bow and arrow and self-defense. One year passed, she had learned a lot from Leo Lee and was very thankful to him. She was ready to face her demons now and talk to Jamie St. Peter's one last time to get some closure for her best friends' death. She booked a flight home to see St Peter's and when she got there she was surprised to see her friends alive— in flesh and blood— right in front of her. She did not know whether she could believe her eyes, whether what she was seeing was real or not.

Chapter 5

Rachel rang the doorbell nervously. She did not know what will she ask St. Peter's, will she even be able to utter words from her mouth? St. Peter's opened the door and welcomed Rachel in. She came in through the door and as soon as she entered she heard a loud noise. She asked St. Peter's what was going on and what was with the noise.

"I have a surprise for you, Rachel," he said.

Eli and I came downstairs. Rachel was shaking to her bones in shock.

"Holy hell! Ahhhh ... zombies!" She screamed and fainted.

"Rachel!" both Eli and I cried as we bent towards the floor. Jamie picked Rachel up and put her on the couch to let her sleep off the shock. As soon she woke up, she saw us looking at her.

She exclaimed, "explain NOW!"

She was very angry— happy to see us, but angry. We told her about the war and what had happened to us. But she could not understand what we were saying. So we had to show her. We took her outside. I went to show on first. I moved towards a log and kept gazing at it as it suddenly caught fire. Then, staightaway I moved towards a bucket full of water and concentrated on it. After a few seconds all the water was out of the bucket floating in the air which I pushed on top of the log to set out the fire. It sizzled as smoke came out of the log. So, I focused once again and wind blew that removed all the smoke from there. Rachel was amazed to see me like that.

She said "Emily I'm so sorry that you must go through all that. I'm never going to leave your side again. I love you, my best friend. It will be okay now."

As soon as she said that, she hugged us both. Next was Eli he was so nervous about his powers because he could not control them yet. He could— he thought to himself— he could hurt Rachel or worse Emily. He did not want to hurt his girlfriend so when he used them he tried his best to control them as much as he could and he hit a tree instead of them. He was relieved that he didn't hurt us.

Chapter 6

Rachel got up early to show Eli and me and what she can do. She said, "I want to show you guys something incredible and I want to tell you all about where I have been in the past year." She took out her bow and arrow, and took us outside with her. She set up the bow and arrow to shoot. She took a breath and aimed for an apple she had put as a target at a far away distance. We were not expecting her to hit it, it was that far. But, she hit the apple. We were amazed at what she can do. She said to us, "it's been a rough year with all that is going on but now I'm glad that we are all together." All of us went inside and she asked us to sit down. She told us what happened with Leo Lee in the mountains. We couldn't believe what she had gone through and the abilities that she has acquired.

Chapter 7

After seeing what Rachel could do, Eli wished he could control his powers better. He went outside for a walk. I knew he was troubled so I asked him if I can I join too. But Eli refused, saying that it can be really cold outside. He went outside talking to himself.

"I have to find a way to control my powers for Emily's sake because I really do love her. I don't want to hurt her."

Eli kept walking with his thoughts and found himself in a park with a bunch of kids. Suddenly he saw a man walking up to him. He started to walk away from the man and noticed that the man was following him. Eli started to run away from him, he even tried to use his powers. But he still could not control them. The man starting to catch up to him. The man caught Eli and pushed him down and pinned him. Then the strange man made Eli inhale a gas to put him to sleep. When Eli woke up, he found himself tied up in an old factory all alone. He screamed "help!" but no one was around. He tried to use his powers but to no avail. While he was struggling to free himself, the same strange man came back and said "I am Dr. Watson and I can help you with controlling your powers."

Eli was startled "how you know about my powers?"

"I've been watching you and that girl of yours for some time now," said Dr. Watson.

"You mean Emily," Eli said.

Dr. Watson chuckled and replied, "yes, so that's her name. She is pretty. I think I'll keep her as a pet all chained up like a dog."

Eli was infuriated. He yelled, "don't you dare touch her!"

"What would you do if I did touch her?"

"I'll kill you myself if you touch her!"

Dr. Watson asked, "would you do anything for her?"

"Yes, I would do anything for her," Eli was quick to answer.

"I see. But what if you end up killing her with your uncontrolled powers?" Dr. Watson continued, "Why don't you try out my invention? It may kill you or change your personality, but you will be able to control your powers more."

"I will do anything for her. I just want to protect her. Even if that means using your stupid invention to control my powers. Yes!" said Eli.

"Good, then you must try this. But remember, it will go in your brain," said Watson.

"I love her and I'd do anything to be by her side, to protect her from creeps like you," affirmed Eli.

Dr. Watson put Eli to sleep and after the operation was finished Eli woke up with a chip in in his head. The operation sure was successful technically and Eli's feeling after the it added to its success. He felt as if he could take over the world. He wanted to go away with Emily; he couldn't stand being at home. He just wished to pick her up and leave his place and disappear from Rachel sight for good and never see her again.

Chapter 8

As soon Eli and I came downstairs, I smacked him in the face and said "where the hell have you been? I've been so worried about you." Eli suddenly yelled "get off my back, woman!" I was shocked at what had just happened. Eli had never spoken to me in that tone. I thought may be he was just tired from being up all night. Little did I know that something had happened to him last night.

Eli roared again, "get me a beer, woman."

"You are acting like a jerk, so stop it or I'll dump you here and now!" I said.

"Fine there's other girls like you."

Emily went upstairs crying. Rachel saw her and went upstairs with Emily and asked what has happened.

"Are you okay, Emily?"

Emily cried and explained everything.

"Oh don't worry. I'll make it better. It will be okay."

Rachel went downstairs to talk to Eli. She urged him to say sorry to Emily.

"Eli! What's the matter with you? Don't you see Emily is in love with you? You fool!" yelled Rachel.

"Come to your wits, woman! She only thinks that because I thought I loved her, but it was only lust of her and I put her feelings for me by using my powers, so shut up! Eli told Rachel everything.

"Eli! How could you? But just say you're sorry to her and I won't hurt you."

Eli laughed and said "you can't hurt me I have powers and you don't."

"Fine I'll take Emily far away from you where you won't find her ever again."

"Take the bitch with you. I don't care about her or you."

"Fine. I'll make her disappear. You will never find her! Ever!"

Rachel went upstairs and spoke to Emily.

"We are leaving. We don't need to deal with his crap."

"Okay I'll pack and say goodbye to Jamie."

Emily said goodbye to Jamie and they left the place promising to start over.

Chapter 9

It had been two months now that Rachel and Emily had left Eli and their country behind. They were in a new land, called Alabrevia. Rachel had found a place where she could bartend and Emily had enrolled herself in a local university.

"So, your classes begin tomorrow. All set to face the horrible professors? You should have just applied at the bar I work at. Life would have been fun and easy," Rachel said.

"Haha! I'd rather learn something new. All fun ends some day afterall."

"Whatever you say! I'm just glad that you are moving on from Eli and his crap."

"Trying to... it still hurts."

"I know, darling. But let's find a man who loves you for the kind hearted woman you are." "Hah! Thanks! I assure you no such man exists. It'll be just us for the rest of our lives. You'll have to grow old with me. Unless of course you find a hottie for yourself."

They continued talking as they fell asleep. The next morning Emily reached her college an hour before the scheduled time just to make sure she is not late on her first day. She entered the premises and looked around. The college building was huge. There was no one around, just empty corridors and classes. Moving around, she found a swimming pool. A man was in it, a very good-looking one Emily thought.

She waved at him and said, "Hi! I'm Emily Jones!".

"I'm Gray Jayden. Nice to meet you!"

Gray came up to the side of the pool and asked Emily, "do you like to swim?"

"I don't know how to."

"Didn't your parents teach you?"

Flashback of her childhood came to Emily. All she could she was her drugged mother who did not have time for anything else, let alone teaching Emily to swim. But, of course, she could not tell this to Gray.

"Well my mom didn't have time for me because she was working late, and my dad died a long time ago."

"Sorry about your dad, but you need to learn to swim. Maybe I can help you too learn to swim if I'm not too busy with my homework and swim class."

"Yeah? Thanks, I appreciate it. You continue, I'll catch you later."

She smiled and walked away.

Chapter 10

Emily continued looking around the college. Suddenly, she bumped into a young man with green hair, but she didn't get his face.

The guy asked, "are you new here?"

Emily replied "yes, I am new here. I'm just looking for the science room and I got lost, but I found the pool room with some guy named Gray in it."

"Oh, yeah I know Gray. He's in my class. He's a popular kid, every girl in this school likes him. By the way, I'm Ben Duke" he said.

"I'm Emily Jones. Nice to meet you, Ben."

"Hey, can I ask you something?" Ben asked hesitantly.

"Yes, sure."

"I would you go out with me, would you? And do you like animals?"

"I just got out of a bad relationship so maybe try again in a couple of months and yes, I love animals."

"So that's a yes."

"Haha! it's a maybe. I must get to know you first."

"I'll take you to the science room now. I think you're in my class."

"Oh, okay thanks, Ben. I hope we can be good friends at least."

Chapter 11

Ben and Emily walked past a couple of classrooms and reached their's. Professor Audre welcomed Emily. After Emily introduced herself to the class, she moved to sit with Ben and Gray, as they were the only two familiar faces in the classroom. But suddenly a female in the classroom waved at her and invited Emily to sit with her. So, she went and sat beside the female.

"Hi, my name is Julia Isabella. Nice to meet you."

"Hey! Yeah likewise," replied Emily.

"So you eye anyone cute here? I am so excited about this new session. I really pray more cuties join us this time." Julia was unabashedly straightforward, unlike Emily.

Emily blushed and said "well... I just got out of a bad relationship so I don't know if any guy is cute. I think I need more time to get over my ex first. Though, Ben isn't bad-looking and Gray is good-looking too. But, no, I don't like them in that way."

"Oh! You have an ex? So what's he like?" asked Julia.

"He was let's just say not the nicest. He always got his way."

"Did he dump you or dump him?"

"Well, he dumped me. Emily replied in a low tone.

"Well, you can find a guy who loves just the way you are," Julia smiled as she said this to Emily.

After talking for a while, the two young women became good friends and Emily slowly got over Eli and what had happened between them.

Chapter 12

After a year I totally forgot about Eli and just spent time with my friends. A school trip was coming up and we were going to the beach. Everyone was excited.

"Yo!" Ben excitedly said, "there will be Women in bathing suits."

"Most likely Emily will be in a bathing suit too," Julia teased Ben, "I know you like her."

"Who are you talking about? I don't know who are you talk about," said Ben.

"Of course Emily Duh! Did you try asking her out yet?" asked Julia.

"Yeah, a year ago but she shot me down. I guess we're just meant to be friends. Besides, she likes Gray just like the rest of the girls in this school. I Have no shot with her anyways."

"How will know if you don't try?" Julia promptly said.

As Emily joined them, Ben thought to himself "yeah, I like Emily, but do I have a chance with her after she told me about her ex that he dumped her for no reason? Should I let her know how I feel or just stay friends? Well I just don't know!"

Emily looked at Ben and said "what's wrong? You have a gloomy face this morning."

"Oh! It's nothing."

Soon, somehow it happened and Ben and I went to town for our date. Gray wasn't too happy about it and he had an eye on us. The difference between Ben and Gray is that I like Gray more because Gray makes me happy. Ben surely knew this. We ate at a restaurant and people kept coming to us saying we were a cute couple and Ben looked really happy about it. After we finished there, we went and roamed on the street. It was a pleasant night. Ben took me by his hand and we went and sat on a bench. We both were all babbles and giggles until Ben started talking about his ex-girlfriend Lily.

"You know, she's dead now."

"Oh my God! I'm sorry... how?"

"She was in a cave and it collapsed."

I felt so sorry for him that I hugged him really tight. After all, I knew what heartbreak meant, and perhaps a sudden death can cause the worst of heartbreaks. But far from my anticipation, Ben shrugged me away.

"Hey! What's wrong? I'm just trying to comfort you."

"Go away, Emily!"

"Hey, it has been long, you should move on now, don't you think so? I know it's difficult but I'm here. I can be your girlfriend."

"I'm going home. Forget this date, Emily!"

After a very long time, I felt connected with someone. I was happy. But he didn't want me and on top of that, he was rude. I couldn't help but cry when I got back to my place. Rachel had noticed that I was upset.

"Hey, what's up? How was your date?"

"Pretty crappy, honestly!"

I told her everything that went by and how I felt. Rachel always knew what to say and what to do.

"Hey! That guy doesn't deserve you. I'll ask him to apologize to you tomorrow, okay?"

"Hm-hm."

"Sleep now."

"Goodnight, Rachel"

"Goodnight, love."

Chapter 13

At the beach I was playing in shallow waters while everybody else played in deeper water.

"Hey, Emily! Come join us!" shouted one of my classmates.

"No, thanks. I'm good here."

I was not upset anymore. I was actually having a good time. But, as soon as I thought I over everything that happened yesterday, Ben came in front of me.

"Hey, Emily" said Ben.

I didn't care that I just wanted him to leave me alone.

"I don't want to see you!" I yelled at him,

"Hey, listen! I'm sorry."

I tried to walk away from Ben. But, he kept blocking my way.

"Ben, how would you have felt if I had been that rude to you? You have felt the same. So please move aside and let me go."

"I'm really sorry, Emily."

"I really can't do this right now, Ben."

Suddenly, he took me by my hand and moved towards the shops at the beach. We did not stop until we reached a place where there were only beach balls around. It was a small hut and nobody was around. I had started to feel sorry for Ben and

I thought may be his emotions got the best of him yesterday. As I was thinking this, both Ben and I moved inside the hut. But to our surprise, Gray and Julia were there. They knew about our tussel, so they at once moved outside the hut. But they locked the door from outside.

"We just want you guys to talk it out. Ping us when everything's sorted. We aren't letting you out before that."

Ben and I, we looked at each other in surprise and then a flurry of laughter burst out of us. We kept looking at each ther for sometime in silence. I hadn't noticed that I had been moving towards him. Ben broke the silence.

"I didn't mean to... really..."

"Shh! That doesn't matter now." As I said this, my lips could not help but move around his.

"This will be our little secret. What do you say, Ben?"

Ben's hands seemed to have agreed at once. He pulled me closer and started kissing me. I kissed him back aggressively. Our hands moved on each other's body, inside and outside our clothes.

"Do you want to...?" I asked.

Ben blushed and said "no!". But his dick had plans of its own. It pressed hard against my thighs.

I couldn't resist myself and started rubbing my hands on it.

"We'll keep it a secret if you want, Ben."

Ben laughed and took off his shirt. He kept caressing my breasts. I took off my bathing suit and stood naked in front of him.

"Wow! You're an angel. Look at these boobies."

He pulled me closer to him at once and started eating them. His lips moved around my nipples. He bit them one by one. I could not hold myself back and I ended up guiding his hand to my vagina. His dick got harder and he put his fingers inside me. We kept kissing each other madly as he kept moving his fingers in and out of me at a pace I had never seen before.

"Ahh.. oh yes, Ben!" is all I kept moaning until he made me cum. I quivered but he did not stop. He sat between my legs as I kept standing there holding the table next to me. His tongue moved rapidly and even swifter were his fingers. He kept fingering and eating me simultaneously as I cummed again. Just as Ben picked me up and put me on the platform, Julia opened the door. Both Ben and I yelled, "no! don't!" We rushed at once and put back our clothes and came out of the hut.

I went along with Julia towards the seashore, leaving Ben behind. Julia and I were playing in the water. She asked me about what went down in the hut. I was about to tell her when suddenly my foot slipped and water pulled me towards the deep side. Julia was trying to get hold of me. She shouted for help. Gray saw us and came running. He jumped right in the sea and pulled me out. I was not breathing but Gray saved my life by giving me a CPR.

Chapter 14

When I woke up, I gaped, and when I saw Gray next to me, I thought to myself, "did Gray save me, why did he do that?"

When Gray woke up and found myself awake he asked, "what happened at the beach?"

"I thought someone pulled my leg in the water and I almost died if you didn't save me. Why did you save me?"

"I think I like you, but I don't know yet I'm not sure yet about my feelings", replied Gray.

"You think you like me? Wait ...I think I like you too. I'm too sure how I feel about you, I want to like you but I just don't want to get hurt again."

Emily kissed him on the check to thank him for saving him. He looked at her and hugged her. "Gray I have something to say" she said. "I won't have any secrets between us okay, so I want to tell you something... I have superpowers."

"What do you mean superpowers? Wait... for real? What do you do?" Gray responded with excitement.

"I'll explain everything when Ben and Julia are around."

"I cant wait. You already are special to me though."

Gray put his lips on Emily's and then they were lost in their world with little care of the superpowers or their friends or Eli and what the world was about to offer them. Gray started kissing her tender neck. She let out a soft moan as he continued to tease her. Before she knew he pulled her bathing suite down to her waist exposing her large breasts and hard perky nipples. He started to lick and tease Emily's nipples and then put the entire nipple in his mouth and sucked on it. It made Emily's pussy instantly wet.

She moaned into Gray's ear, "please lick my pussy right now. I am so wet."

Gray hurriedly removed Emily's bathing suit. He made her spread her legs and started licking her beautiful shaved pussy madly. She moaned as she pressed his faced between her legs. She moaned loudly every time gray's tongue touched her engorged clitoris. After a few minutes he inserted a finger into her wet vagina and focused his tongue on her rock-hard clit. After about 10 minutes, she had already had 6 orgasms. She was panting and wanting more with a massive wet spot on the ground. Emily sat up and kissed gray hard on the lips telling him to fuck her hard. Gray smiled like a Cheshire cat and slowly inserted his hard cock into Emily's dripping wet pussy. She pulled him closer as he thrust in and out hitting her g-spot, making her moan louder. It didn't take long before both Gray and Emily were on the cusp of cumming.

Chapter 15

After the beach trip we all returned to school and went to attend our classes. The entire trip now almost seemed like it was a dream. I was walking in the corridor when I heard a couple of student talking about the head-chef in our school, that he was a retired superhero. I asked around a couple of students and got to know that this was a popular notion among students. Having known that superpowers are real, I was very intrigued. Later that day, I appealed to my classmates' boredom that followed the trip and suggested that we have a cooking competition against the school schef, a cook off.

The chef's name was Scott William but some people called him Iron Chef. Emily thought it was a good idea to not see Gray for a while since he knows about her powers and her feelings towards him. Gray was puzzled at this behaviour. Gray thought to himself "is Emily mad at me? I guess so since I didn't give her an answer of what I think about her. But, I still like her. I don't care if she has powers or not. I want to be with her but how can I tell her that?" So when Emily was in the cafetaria Emily challenging Scott to a cook off, Gray passed a note to Julia to give to Emily. It said 'I'm sorry that I acted like a jerk. I still like you and I want to be with you if you have me as your boyfriend. I will accept your powers if you accept me being a jerk sometimes.'

Chapter 16

Emily had challenged Scott to a battle. Scott agreed to it on terms that the loser has to clean the dishes for a week. Terms were announced in the entire school and everybody was excited. Emily was thinking about what to dish to choose. What is it that she can make best? As she was lost in her thoughts, Julia gave her Gray's note. Emily, as unsure as she was about all boys in her life at the moment, decided not to think about anyone. She was focused on the competition. She must cook and win.

The tables were set for the cook-off. On the left was Emily and on the right table was Scott. Emily prepared a steak with grilled onion and Scott made pork ribs with potatoes on the side. Both the dishes look splendid. The five judges came to their tables and tasted each of their dishes. Emily and Scott both were nervous and everybody was eagerly waiting for the results. Who will do the dishes for the coming week? Will Emily find out more about Scott?

Chapter 17

Emily had planned to tell Ben and Julia about her powers right after the cooking-battle. She also had to reply to Gray's note. She had to make it clear to both Ben and Gray that she liked them both. But first was the battle.

She was waiting for the results clinching her hands. The results came in, and it was a tie. The judges decided that each of their dishes tasted equally good, had the perfect flavour and texture. After he said that, Emily wanted to tell Ben and Julia about her powers first. She was going to tell them everything about her powers, and how she got them. Then she would respond to Gray's note. She will tell them how she feels about Ben and Gray, that she likes them both.

In the kitchen, Emily told Julia and Ben about the cook-off. The judges for the cook battle had tasted their food and both of their dishes tasted good. Therefore, it was a tie.

"Both of us won. So, I and Scott decided to share the dishes."

But first she needed to tell her friends about her powers.

She sits beside them and says, "I need to talk to you guys, there's something that I should have told you when all of us met for the first time. First, I have Element powers. Gray knows that I have powers. I told him about them. The second thing is that I like Ben and Gray at the same time, but I don't know If Ben can accept that I have super powers or not. I know how I feel about them and I don't want anyone to be scared of me."

Chapter 18

After what I said to them, they were quite shocked. If they need time, I'll give them time to think it over. I will have to show them my powers to make them understand. Then, they will decide to accept me the way I am or not. I take them outside, away from the school.

It could get very dangerous if Emily loses her focus on what she is doing. They go to the soccer field where Emily can show them her powers. She shows them water first, then earth, next was air and the last was fire.

Emily warns them, "You guys have to get some distance between you all and me. I don't want to hurt you with my fire."

Chapter 19

I showed them fire but they weren't impressed. They were very scared of me. They said that they hate me and I am a freak, but it was out of fear.

I ran away crying because my so-called friends did not accept me. Gray ran after me.

As he ran after me, he bumped into someone and hurriedly said, "I'm sorry I bumped you."

Eli smiled and said, "It's okay." Then he walked along.

I saw Eli standing in the hall way. I went upto him and railed, "What the fuck! What are you doing here Eli?"

Eli said, "I miss you, Emily. I'm sorry that I was a bit of a dick when we broke up. Can we start over?"

I yelled on top of my voice, "Piss off! Fuck no! Last time you said you could get a girl just like me, so fuck you, Eli! Please go to hell. I started a new life away from you and your bullshit."

"You bitch! I'll turn all your so-called new life upside down."

"It is already messed up enough. How can you make it worse?"

Eli now saw Gray, standing a few feet behind me.

Chapter 20

Once Eli saw Gray, he asked who he was.

Emily said, "He's my boyfriend, and no, we aren't dating yet. But I would like to be with him if he will have me as his girlfriend."

She smiles at Gray.

Racked with jealousy, Eli picked him up with his powers and tried to kill Gray. Emily intervenes with her fire powers and tells Gray to run.

"Get to the school and hide. I'll take care of Eli."

Eli asks, "How are you going to take care of me, Emily?"

"I'm going to fight you, you dumb shit. You tried to kill my friend and you tried to ruin my life. So, fuck you!"

Using her powers, Emily fights Eli, to protect her only friend and maybe lover.

Eli goes after Gray to find out what he was to her. Eli asks him, "Who are you? What's going on between you and Emily?"

Gray tells Eli that he might be her future boyfriend and maybe someday her husband.

"I am in love with Emily", said Gray, "and there is nothing you can do about it!"

Full of rage, Eli used his powers on Gray. Emily yelled at Eli and put him down with her powers.

"I'll fight you but leave Gray alone. He's my boyfriend. Please don't hurt him. I'll fight you, and if I win, you will leave and never come back."

Emily looked at him with hatred in her eyes. She was going to fight him on Monday after school.

Chapter 21

Monday arrived and we gathered in the soccer ground after school.

While I fought with Eli, there were cameras that filmed us fighting. I threw a lot of dirt at him and spat, "For all the shit that comes out of your mouth". Then I used the wind as I said, "For all the backstabbing you do."

I rained down water on him for being an asshole to me and Rachel for years. I used fire on him for not being there for us when we needed him most.

The fight went on and on.

I knew I was going to finish him as the end neared. I was close to putting an end to all the hell that he put me through for years, but Gray came out of hiding and hugged me.

He said, "Don't kill him, Emily. I know he put you through a lot but don't kill him."

I reassured Gray, "I'll hurt Eli. I will make sure he never comes near us again."

I broke Eli's arm and warned him, "Do not ever come here again or I'll kill you. If you come near me or my boyfriend again, you're a dead man. You fucking hear me, asshole? You come near us and I'll kill you for real. Gray will not stop me next time!"

Chapter 22

After the fight was over and Eli left the school, I fainted from exhaustion.

Gray picked me up and carried me to the school infirmary to take care of me. He lets me sleep it off.

He thinks to himself, Emily has been through alot in her life but I can help her put Eli in her past. I hope to be her future.

I wake up to find Gray looking at me.

I tell him, "I want to sleep with you!"

He asks me, "In what way?"

"I want you to fuck me."

He lay down beside me and we begin to make love.

I take off my shirt and then remove his T-shirt. He takes his pants off and his underwear and begins to kiss me passionately. Pausing for a moment, Gray says, "I love you Emily." I say it back to him, "I love you too, Gray." He kisses me with passion and slides his penis in my pussy. I start to moan in pleasure. He says, "yes, yes", breathlessly and I tell him to put it in deeper. As he thrusts his penis deeper into my pussy, I cum and yell at Gray, "Fuck me like a beast, Gray. Fuck me like you would fuck no one else." I cum again as he picks me up and pins me against the wall. He fucks me against the wall and I cum hard. Then he lays me onto the couch. We fuck on the couch and Gray says, "I'm going to cum." I moan and tell him, "Just cum. I can't take more." He cums right in my pussy.

We lie on the couch together, exhausted and satisfied.

Ben saw them together. It made him real sad that he didn't accept her powers like Gray did. Now he has lost the woman he liked, maybe even loved. But he couldn't be with her anymore, now that she's with Gray.

Chapter 23

Having showered in the school shower, they put their clothes back on.

Gray asks Emily "Are we dating now?"

Emily acquiesces, "Yes, we are".

Gray beamed. He was so happy to love some one like her. He felt that he could take on the world now.

In class, every one was talking about Emily and her amazing powers, and how she had kicked Eli's ass. Her classmates came up to her and asked so many questions. They wanted to know who was the guy she had fought. She informed them that he was her ex-boyfriend.

They showed her a video of her kicking some real ass. In the video, she was fighting him and had the balls to threaten to kill him if he came back. Her classmates asked her if she will protect them from evil villains?

"Emily, will you protect us?"

"Yes, I will", she promised. She was Element, chosen to save the people of Alabrevia.

"This is my city now. No one will destroy my city or harm my people while I am alive. I will be your hero."

Chapter 24

Eli goes back to Dr Watson and narrates all that had happened between him and Emily. Eli complains that he wanted a strong team to kill Emily and her so-called friends.

He hates how good she has become. He misses the old Emily who loved going to war. He remembers the look on her face when was about to kill the enemy. She showed no mercy. That is why I loved her so much.

But she is too good for him now. I can't have her anymore. She must die.

Firstly, I have to heal these cuts and bruises before I can see her again. In the meantime, Dr Watson can put together a team for Eli.

Eli instructs Dr Watson, "Get me a guy named Todd Tucker, and his whore of a girlfriend Emma Star. His power is that he is a pussy ticker but he's a real wimp of a man. He doesn't like to fight with any one but loves to hit on women who are taken. His grilfriend's power is attracting men and putting them in their place or merely sleeping with them."

Dr Watson found Todd and Emma. He promised to introduce them to Eli once his wounds had healed from his fight with his ex-girlfriend. "He will be your team leader", said Dr Watson.

They laughed at him.

"What? Our leader? A weekly who gets beat up by a woman!" They thought Eli was really weak because he had been beat up by a woman.

Dr Watson explained how powerful Emily was.

"She can control the elements. She could be like a bomb going off or a windstorm. She will be hard to kill but it is possible. I have found a way to kill her with a red rock. I call it 'ani element'. It will take away her powers and slowly kill her."

Chapter 25

Sometime after Emily was dubbed a hero and protector of Alabrevia city, she called Rachel and told her everything. How Eli came back and what happened in the fight with him. How she is a hero now. How she kicked Eli's ass to hell and back. Also, she has a new boyfriend now. Once Emily was done talking to Rachel, she decided to join the school. Rachel would join Emily's class to protect her best friend from getting hurt by that asshat of a guy, and to meet her new boyfriend as well.

Chapter 26

When Rachel joined the school, Ben started to hit on her right away. He asked her if she will be his girlfriend? Of course, he got shot down.

Rachel scolded him, "I won't go out with you because you hurt my best friend. So what if she has powers? You had no right to say that you hate her. Sure, it's scary to see them. But to say that you hate her? What the fuck man! That's not cool."

"I hear there is a new sous chef", said Julia. "I think his name was Francis Louie. I hear he's hot, single and can cook. What a man!"

"Well, I hear he's a ninja that ran away from home to be a chef! Let's go meet him", said Emily. "Maybe if he's nice, we could be friends with him?"

All of them went to meet Francis and introduce themselves. Gray looked really jealous. He thought of Emily like he owned her. He decided to kiss Emily right in front of Francis. The look that Francis gave him was a nasty one but then, a girl came up to Gray out of nowhere.

It was Emma.

Emily thought, that whore of a girlfriend of Todd's goes to this school?

Emma squeaked, ""Hi ya Gray, baby how are you doing? When are we going out again? I miss you!"

Emily wanted to kill Gray at that moment. Emily slaps Gray right across his face.

"Don't ever talk to me again! WE ARE OVER! I DON'T SLEEP AROUND WITH OTHER MEN LIKE YOU DO!"

She runs away crying and feeling hurt. Broken and upset, she runs away to the park to think.

Francis runs after her and finds her sitting on the swings, crying her eyes out. He feels sorry for her.

She was using her powers but she didn't know she was using them. When Francis found her in the park, he could not believe what he saw. Was Emily really Element, whom the news channels are calling the new super hero on TV?

He asked her, "Are you okay?"

Between sobs she said, "I broke up with my boyfriend."

"Why?"

"He cheated on me with a whore."

"You don't need to cry over that jerk. You are beautiful, in your own way."

"Thanks," said Emily and smiled at him, kissing him on the cheek.

"I have a question," he said.

"What's up?", Emily asked.

"Are you Element?"

She did not reply. Would she hurt him if she said yes? Would he accept me as I am?

Chapter 27

A year had passed, and Emily had not told Francis whether she was Element or not.

Emily thought to herself, I liked him. I kept all that to myself. Yeah, I know he needs to know, if I want to date him. But can I trust him to keep it a secret untill I say so?

Well, I don't know if he likes me or not. What if he doesn't? Then I'll look like an idiot with every one watching?

Or do I go out with Gray again? Yeah, no. Fuck that idea. I'd rather kill myself than be with that cheating jerk.

Maybe I'll tell him how I feel about him. Then see what happens ... but how can I say that I like him when I don't know if he even likes me back? Maybe I can get one of my friends to do it. What if he has a girlfriend? Then what? I'll be hurt and broken all over again. I'll have no boyfriend to protect me or someone I could protect.

Okay Emily, get yourself together!

She was talking to herself before the mirror in the women's bathroom at school. As she came out, she ran into Francis out in the hall.

He said, "Hi Emily".

Emily blushed and ran away, wondering if he heared me talking to myself just now? What does he think of me now? OH MY GOD! If he heard me, then he knows I like him. OH SHIT.

Chapter 28

I really wanted to know if Francis had overheard me talking to myself before the bathroom mirror. Does he know that I like him? Maybe I'll just ask him about it or get one of my friends to do it?

I decided that I'll ask Rachel to do it. I went up to her asked her, "Rachel, can you ask Francis if he overheard me talking to myself in the bathroom?"

"Emily! Do you like Francis?"

"Aaaa maybe... okay yes, just don't tell anyone okay. Not even Julia. No one. Okay?

"Emily, I'll talk to him about it okay."

"Thanks! You're the best Rachel."

"I know I am, only for you, my best friend."

"I love you."

"I know you do. I love you too. You know that I'd do anything for you, right?", said Rachel. "Yeah, I know."

"I'll go talk to your crush now!", teased Rachel.

Rachel teased me about liking Francis now, as friends do. I blushed and quickly retorted, "He's not my crush! Are we in high school or what? Maybe I like him a little. That doesn't mean I am crushing on him!"

When Rachel got to the café were Francis works hard at his job, she snuck up to him and asked, "Did you hear Emily in the bathroom talking to herself?"

"Yeah, I did. Why are you asking me that?"

"Did you hear the part that she likes you?"

"What? Emily likes me?"

"Yes, she is crushing on you hard time."

"Oh?"

"Do you like her back?"

"Yeah, I do, but you can't tell her that okay. I don't want our friendship to be over just because I like her."

"Are you going to ask her out or not?"

"I'm not sure how to ask her out yet. I did see something that was kind of a shock."

"What was it?"

"I saw Emily using her powers, but I wasn't scared of her. I was fascinated by her all the more. That's one of the reasons I started to like her. She is very beautiful and as I got to know her, the more I liked her. Maybe, someday I will be in love with her and we will be happy together."

"How will you ever know if you never try? You have to ask her out first and see what happens."

"Yeah, but what if she says no to me?"

"She won't. She really likes you. You have nothing to worry about. But it didn't come from me okay, if you are going to ask her out!"

"First, I think she needs to know about my past. Then we will see about asking her out."

Chapter 29

Francis was looking for Emily to talk to her about his past, but he just couldn't find her.

Emily wasn't any where. She wasn't in the gym or in the bathroom? Where can she be? Emily was hiding in a garbage can in the café, where he finally found her.

Puzzled, Francis asked her, "Why are you hiding in the garbage can, Emily?"

"It was the only place you wouldn't look", Emily answered.

Francis thought to himself, she is the weirdest person I have met so far. I like that she's cool, kind, strong, beautiful, weird, and has powers.

He just could not hold it in any more and all of a sudden, he kissed her, right in front of everyone.

Emily was taken aback. She was like, "What just happened?"

Francis said, "I have liked you for over a year now. Will you go out with me?"

Emily was very quiet for a moment. Then she acquiesced, "Yes, I will."

She was so happy she hugged him and he hugged her right back.

"But if we are to date Emily, I need to tell you about my past first, okay?"

"I'll tell you about mine, too."

I began telling Francis about my past, about why Eli is stalking me and what he did to me. But then, I thought, let's start from the beginning. When I was kid, my mom was a dug addict. I didn't know who my dad was until I was 18. I went into foster care and I got adopted by a nice old man by the name of Jamie but he died 5 years later. I was 10 at the time and I was adopted by a team named Power Girls. I think they felt sorry for me and adopted me. Anyways, I know it's a stupid name but they were good people. Years later, I left them to join the army when I was 18. Through the army, I met my best friends Rachel and Eli. I was part of a Black Ops Team in the war. I recounted all of this for Francis.

He narrated his own past to me.

"I was a leader of a secret ninja society, but I wanted to explore the world and follow my passion for cooking. My parents were killed when I was a child. I have been chasing the same group that killed my parents for 20 years since I was kid."

Chapter 30

The more they talked, the more Francis liked her. Maybe he would even fall for her. When he asked her out, he didn't know what to do. Then he had an idea to make Emily fall for him. As a sous chef, he can really cook. Therefore, he will show her what he can do in the kitchen. He invited Emily to dinner at his house.

When she shows up, he was cooking up a storm with his ninja techniques, showing off just a little to impress her. He was going to cook her some steak and lobster, steamed veggies with a cream sauce.

She smiles at him like she really likes him. But he is not sure how much she likes him. She whispers, "I love you", but he doesn't hear it. He is busy cooking, the clatter of the pots and pans too loud for him to hear it. A sad look settles on her face. Francis asks, "What's wrong, Emily?"

Giving him a fake smile as if something was on her mind, she says, "It's nothing." Francis doesn't say anything but right after dinner, Emily takes him by the hand and pulls him towards the bed.

She starts kissing him fervently and they get into bed together. Francis kisses Emily's neck passionately, while his hands explored her body. It wasn't long before Emily 's shirt and bra were off and Francis was suckling on her hard erect nipples. She moaned with pleasure as he flicked them with his tongue. Before she knew it, he was kissing a trail which crept lower. Quickly, he pulls her pants and panties off.

Francis had his head buried in between Emily's legs, flicking his tongue hard and fast on her engorged clit and dripping pussy. She arches her back and moans loudly as she has a massive orgasm, squirting everywhere passionately.

Francis takes her clothes off slowly and kisses her back until they are both naked on his bed. Getting on top of her, he puts his dick in her pussy and starts to have sex with her. It was different this time. It felt like real love this time. Gray wasn't like this with her.

When they were done, they showered together. Francis kissed her in the shower. She asked him, "Are we dating yet?"

He looked at her and repeated a question he had asked her once before, "Are you Element?"

"Can I trust you?"

"Yes, of course you can."

"Then yes, I am. I have powers. I can control the elements. That's why I am called Element."

He was in shock. The woman he might be in love with has powers. What can be done now?

Chapter 31

The next morning I was felt sick. It seemed like I had the flu, so I decided to look it up. It was a pregnancy symptom. I freaked out and went to the drug store to get a test. Once I had got it, I peed on it and waited. Within 5 seconds, the test results appeared. I had tested positive.

Oh Shit! Wait, can a super hero get pregnant?, I thought to myself. I have to tell Francis first.

Once I am back in his house, I go to his room and wake Francis up. I have something to tell him, only him.

"Okay mmmm..."

"Francis, I need to tell you something and show you something as well."

"Do you know what time it is?"

"I know it's early but I need to show you something."

I show him the test and say, "I'm pregnant."

I was sure that Francis was the father of the baby.

"What you want to do about it?", I ask him. "Do you want to keep it or not?"

"I always wanted to have kids with the woman I love. When I met you, I thought you were the most beautiful woman I have met by far and now you will have my baby. I'm happy to meet you Emily because the truth is, I... lo—never mind."

Francis thought to himself, she would never say she loves me. I'm a monster. I have killed people. But she is having my baby so that's that.

"Emily, will you be my girlfriend since you are having my baby?"

"Yes, I will be." I smile at him.

"So, we are dating now and you are having my baby."

"Yup, we are."

She smiled at him like she was ready to fall in love with him. Francis asked her, "Are you in love with me?"

"No, we just started dating."

She lies to him about not being in love with him, but she is. She doesn't want to tell him yet.

Chapter 32

Rumours about Francis and me dating spread through school. Since I was pregnant, as the other girls walked by me, they said real rude things. They said, I was a slut. The guys were saying that he raped me and got me pregnant.

Eli heard about it through Emma who was in my school. The rumours would go on until I went to that school.

Eli wanted to save me and my unborn baby. He was worried that we would became a family. When he got there, I stopped him at the door.

"Eli! WHY THE FUCK ARE YOU HERE?", I said. "I warned you I'd kill you if you came back. The reason I'm not killing you right now is because I don't want to hurt my unborn child but my boyfriend will try to kill you. He is a ninja."

"I thought he raped you and got you pregnant."

"Are you stupid, Eli? He is my boyfriend."

When I told him that, his heart broke in two pieces. When he heard that, he picked me up with his power and tried to kill me but Francis showed up.

"Hey, asshat! Put her down!"

Eli tried to strangle me with his powers. He shouted at Francis, "Go to hell! I'm going to kill her. Then no one will touch her ever again. I'll make sure her body is preserved so she stays the way she is. No other man will touch her again."

"Like hell I'm going to let you kill my future wife and the woman who is the mother of my child. Like hell I'm going to let you kill her asshole. If you dare to try to kill her, I'll kill you myself bastard! Emily are you okay? I'll get you down okay. Then I'll say what I should have said when I said I lo.. I'll finish it. I promise I won't hesitate to say it this time."

"I'm okay. Go kill Eli. He must die. I know it's wrong to say that but he has been a pain in my ass ever since I met him. He thinks I'll forgive him and take him back. What a joke! He must be delusional. Babe, you must kill him."

I really wanted Eli dead.

Francis pulled out a knife and stabbed Eli right in his gut. Immediately, Emily was set free.

She said to Francis, "Babe, pin him down for me."

"Baby, are you sure?"

She looked right at Eli like she really was going to kill him.

She said to Eli, "Thank you fo all the crap you have put me through. You broke my heart but without you dumping me, I wouldn't have met my boyfriend and the love of my life. So, I thank you, Eli. You made me the woman I am today but you need to die. Don't worry, I'll make sure your body is turned to ash by using my powers. Get ready."

Emily used her fire powers as Eli screamed for mercy for her to stop. As he was burning, he cried out, "Now, that's the Emily I know and love. The Emily who showed no mercy to her enemies."

I tell him to go to hell.

"Eli, I don't want to be this person anymore."

She puts out the fire and shows him mercy but Francis does not. He lifts up a rock and hits Eli in the head with it over and over until he's a lifeless corpse.

Francis had killed Eli. It was finally over. Emily was free of Eli's bullshit. She could go on living with Francis and her friends.

Chapter 33

After Eli was dead, Francis said something to me. "Will you marry me, Emily?"

I said, "Yes."

He went down on his knees and pulled out a ring. Suddenly, a woman showed up and said, "I love you Francis. I want to be your wife. Will you marry me?"

He said, "No, of course not."

"I love you Emily and you are the mother of my child. I'm going to take you to my ninja village. She doesn't need this crap of bullshit rumours and jealous women. We will be married there and have our child there too. We will live there and no one will ever find us. We will tell Rachel and the others where we are going. You can't stop us, random person I don't know."

The woman implored Francis, "My name is Sukura Olivia. I'm in your cooking class Francis."

Emily said to her, "Okay. Sukura, is it? Listen. Francis is my man, okay? You need to back off, woman."

As I glared at her, she got scared of me and ran off.

Francis said, "Now that she is gone, let's start where we left off, okay? Emily, will you marry me? I love you."

I said, "Yes. I love you too."

We got married in his village, where I gave birth to our daughter Lilyanna jone Louie. And we lived happy ever after.

THE END? OR IS IT? Stay and watch the unfolding saga of their daughter picking up the slack of her parents.

Book 2 of Element: Electra

By

Lindsay Warkentin and David Leahy

PROLOGUE

My name is Lilyanna jone Louie. I am the daughter of Emily and Francis Louie. You may also know them by their hero names—Element and Ninja Chef. He is the one who killed my mom's ex-boyfriend with a rock. I did not have any powers until I was older. I had no clue why people are after me and my family. I think they started coming after us once my brother Zack was born. He wouldn't remember this. He was just a baby. This is my story. How we had to run from the league of assholes and how I got my powers just like my mom and dad.

When I got my powers, it was my 12th birthday party. My brother kept crying more and more until—yup, you guess it—electricity flowed out of my hands. I thought being a ninja kid was cool but every one was really surprised when electricity came out of my hands.

This is just the beginning of what is to come in the future.

Chapter 1

After my party ended and my parents had taken Zack to bed, a random man broke into our outhouse. My parents fought him off but my mom took it too far and set the house on fire. Zack was kidnapped by the unknown man, who was Todd as we later found out.

I was thinking to myself, well, my brother is kidnapped and my mom has set our house on fire. Like what the fuck Mom? I am going to bring him back. Even if it takes years, I will bring him home.

"Mom! Dad! I have an idea. What if I get Zack back? But it might take me a very long time to get him."

My mom said to me, "Honey, that would be too dangerous."

"But mom", I said to her, "I want to go, please let me go."

My mom turned to my dad and asked, "Should we let her go to get our son back with us?"

My dad said to me, "Sweetie, we will let you go if you take your mother's power gloves with you. Take the communicator to keep in touch with us once every week. Go to see aunt Rachel. She will train you and help you with the powers that you've got."

So, I packed my things and set out on my journey to find my brother and get him home safe.

Chapter 2

After getting off the plane, I walked out of the airport and saw aunt Rachel. I told her what had happened to Zack, how he was kidnapped and how our mom had set the house on fire. All she did was laugh at me about my mom setting the house on fire.

She said, "Yup. That's your mom for you. But we will get your brother back. I'll help you find your brother and show you how to control your powers. You can be far more powerful than you are now, Lilyanna. Are you ready to train and get your brother back from the assholes that took him?"

Chapter 3

I trained with my aunt for 8 years. I had developed new powers like ice and fire powers. I can control lightning with my electric powers.

Rachel said to me, "If you want to fight for your brother, you will need a cool costume to go with your powers. I can make you something but you will have to wait for a bit."

"Thank you so much, aunt. I will wait for what you come up with! I AM SO EXCITED TO SEE IT!"

So, Aunt Rachel went to work on my power suit. A few days later, Aunt Rachel announced, "It's done!"

The power suit looked like a mini dress. It was red and black in colour, with some ninja tools stitched on its side. I tried it on and it really looked fabulous on me but there is something missing in it. My mom's power gloves do not match the suit at all but Aunt Rachel tells me, "Here, I made you some black power gloves of your own."

"I can't wait to show my parents this suit. I love it, thank you so much, Aunt Rachel."

"If you want to get your brother back, you might need some help to do it."

Chapter 4

I spoke to my parents on the communicator about my suit and they were very proud of me. I was thinking about spying on the league of assholes to see what their plans are for my brother and if they plan to bring my mom's ex-boyfriend Eli back to life.

I asked aunt Rachel about spying on the league of assholes as I was wondering about what their plans are.

"DON'T DO THAT!" She yelled at me and said, "Let me see your communication."

I said, "Okay?"

I let her see my communication. She too listens to their communication to see their plans without going to their hideout. No one knows where they are, so Aunt Rachel listens to what they are saying.

Chapter 5

As my aunt and I listen to the league of assholes' conversation on the communicator, we find out about their plans. What we were listening to was crazy. They really planned to try to bring Eli back from the dead. I was just thinking out loud to myself.

We heard a woman yelling at one of the guys saying, "I WANT ELI BACK! JUST FIND A WAY TO DO THAT!"

After searching, they might have found a way to bring Eli back from the dead. There is a fountain of youth which could bring Eli back from the dead. However, there is a catch. The fountain is cursed. If we go there, it might not be Eli whom we bring back. It could just as well be a demon or something much worse than Eli. If Eli and a demon are put together, Eli could be cursed. Every death will always be a living death. A Zombie.

"Do you want that for him?", said one of the workers to the bossy woman.

"I don't care about that. I want my Eli back. I just miss him."

She blushes thinking about Eli. How he was so cold to her. How he hated Emily. Well, we got her brat baby boy with us and he is slowing turning evil just like Eli was. We just need to see his potential, just need to push him but how? Hmm... wait, doesn't the brat have an older sister? Maybe we can kidnap her, see if she breaks.

"Hey! stupid woman", said Todd, "she doesn't have powers like her mother. I couldn't defeat her and that stupid asshole of a boyfriend of hers. They might even be married by now and that boy is my boy. Shut your bitch mouth, Emma.

Chapter 6

Emma said to him, "He's my boy too, you know. I might not have given him life but he's still our son. That won't change. I love our Zacky poo, you know that Todd."

"As much as you love Eli?"

"WHAT? I don't love Eli! The only man I love is you, only you."

"Why do you sleep with other men if you love me?", he yelled at her.

She yelled back, "I do that because you make me. I'm not like that. You bring it out of me! You can be an asshole if you are my asshole. I love you, Todd. Why do you think I don't love you?"

"I saw you when you were talking to the workers. I saw you blush Emma. So, let me ask you this. Emma do you want to fuck Eli, our leader, who needs our help right now because he is dead? Right now we need to bring him back from the dead. So, Emma, what will it be? Do you want to fuck Eli? Is it just that or do you love him?"

"I don't really know what love is. I don't know if you and I have that because I let you fuck me every night. I thought I need you but maybe I was wrong about you Todd. I thought we would be married by now and live our life away from Eli and his bullshit, with Emily and her family.

"Emma, it's over. Pack your things and leave. You will always be a slut."

"Fine. But I'm taking our son with me, MOTHER FUCKER. So, fuck you and fuck Eli. I hope he stays dead or becomes a zombie."

Chapter 7

"I need Zack to wake up the Dragon. So, you can go fuck yourself woman. Goodbye bitch." As soon as she left, she bumped into Zack. He called to her, "Mama, are you leaving?"

"I'll be back to get you, okay? You are my sweet but evil boy. I love you so very much Zack." She touches his check and kisses him goodbye, leaving the league of assholes behind.

She planned to get even with Todd. She would get Eli back by herself and tell him everything that Todd has been up to. But she will need Eli's body first. It is in the hide out. She goes inside the hide out and retrieves Eli's body, taking it with her to the fountain of youth. Emma puts Eli's body in the fountain and sees some life coming back in Eli's face.

It's working, she thought to herself. As the cold wind blew, Eli got up and was really quiet at first. But when she asked him, "Eli, are you okay?", he said "Yes, I'm just fine."

She smiled and cried.

"I missed you very much Eli. I have to tell you about Todd. He kidnapped a baby boy and the boy is now 8 years old. He has the power to wake up a monster and he can heal or kill any one he wants. Todd is planning to wake up a dragon to kill Emily and her family. With the dragon's powers, he might be able to kill Emily. Do you want Emily dead, Eli?"

"No", he said, "I want to destroy her."

"There's one more thing. The boy is Emily's son but we needed him, so, we kidnapped him. Now, he thinks Todd is his dad. Can you please talk him out of this dragon nonsense? He broke up with me but he might listen to you. He thinks that I'm in love with you, but he's wrong. Please, just talk to him Eli."

"Oh, I'll talk to him. Then I'll kill him, take the kid and wake up the dragon myself. First, I think I'll kill you, since you're here."

He used his powers to choke her until she stopped breathing. Then, he snapped her neck and threw her into the fountain of youth. She woke up and cursed him, "You asshole, you killed me."

"Sorry. I need someone like me so I had to kill you. I need you to be a part of my plan. That's why I killed you. So, Todd kidnapped Emily's son, huh? Sounds interesting."

Chapter 8

They arrived at the hide out together. Eli ordered Emma, "To get Zack from Todd and wake up the dragon, we just need to see where he is sleeping. Now, go get the boy."

Todd saw Emma carry Zack in her arms and not only that, Eli was with her too. Wasn't he dead or did she go to the fountain of youth to bring him back to life? She looks dead herself. She looks pale, like she died and Eli brought her back to life at the fountain of youth. But isn't it cursed? Todd was thinking to himself.

"How are you, Eli? I mean, how are you back from the dead?", said Todd.

Eli yelled at him, "WHY THE FUCK DID YOU TAKE EMILY'S KID! You stupid jackass! You didn't think what would happen once the dragon comes back to life, kills the kid and sends his body to his bitch of a mother? That bitch and the boyfriend she married are going to pay for killing me. He's going to get destroyed for helping her kill me. We need to hurry up and find the dragon, so that we can send it after Emily to destroy her family and everything she stands for."

Chapter 9

"I will come after them. I will show them that I'm not afraid of them. I'll show them the true meaning of being afraid of something in this world. We will find this dragon and when we do, we will send it to Emily's village and let it destroy everything she and her family stands for."

Trying to find the dragon on the websites online did not come up with any luck. So, they had to steal the Book of Monsters.

Emma said to Eli, "The last time I saw this book, it was in a church. I think the Power Girls have the book. It's heavily guarded with laser and shit."

Eli creepily smiled at her and said, "That's my girl. Always thinking on her feet. That is why I picked you to join my army of the undead, Emma."

Emma thought to herself, did Eli say that I was his Girl? Or was it wishful thinking?

They began looking up churches where the Power Girls might be. Finally, they got to know that the book was hidden in a church by the name of St. Ignatius Church, in the city for years. "That's where the book is. We are going to take it from them tonight," said Emma, all smart and knowing.

So, Eli, Emma and Todd went to steal the Book of Monsters. Emma had to use her powers to get the guards to leave their post but one problem came up. Once inside, she found out that the guards were women. She couldn't use her powers on them. So, Todd came up to them and asked them where the bathroom was? Todd was trying to get them to leave their post, just for a sec, so Emma and Eli could get the book.

Chapter 10

After sneaking into the room where the book was being kept, they went to grab it but the alarm went off. The camera was on them and Eli quickly used his powers and took off with Emma. They jumped out of the window, taking the book with them and ran as fast as they could to the hideout.

When the guards came back from the men's bathroom with Todd, they noticed that the door was broken into. They went into the room and saw that the book was taken. One of the guards said, "Call the Power Girls now! The Book of Monsters has been stolen."

A guard phoned the power girls and—yup you guessed it—the Power girls got hold of Emily and Francis to ask for their help. Of course, both agreed to help them. They were the first group to let Emily in, before she left them to go to war ten years ago. If she hadn't gone, she would never have found her powers and become Element.

"It's because of it that Eli isn't with us. Otherwise, maybe he wouldn't be evil and we wouldn't have killed him," said Emily on the phone with the Power Girls.

"But I can't believe he is back from the dead. I don't know how they did it, but he came back."

"Well, it looks like we must kill Eli again," said Francis to his wife. She laughed, and willingly agreed.

Chapter 11

My parents tried very hard to find the league of assholes but they were nowhere to be found. How were they going to stop them from bringing a Dragon back to this world? Then my dad said, "I think there's an old abandoned ninja base nearby. We could look at it. It might give us a clue to our baby."

My mom told him that they could look at it on their way back. "Our Zack may not be there. Our Lilyanna is looking for him as well and may need some help doing so. When we get back, let's phone up our old friends and see what they can do to help her out. Let's just find the Book of Monsters now and put it where Eli and his no-good followers can't reach.

When my parents went to the ninja base, there was no one there. But why was someone standing near the door? They went to take a closer look and suddenly found themselves falling through a TRAP DOOR. Now, Emily and Francis needed to be saved from Eli and his no-good followers.

Chapter 12

When they fell to the ground, my mom used her fire powers to light up the room. The found themselves trapped in a cage with electric wires crisscrossing all around them. My parents tried to get out of the cage but they got shocked by it. That's when Eli came out of the shadows.

"Well, well. Look what the cat dragged in? Some noisy rats trying to ruin my plans for the becoming of the Dragon Borea. He's going to destroy everything you and your family stand for. Maybe I'll have you as my undead minion. Then you would have to fight your own daughter in the end. Now, that'd be funny," said Eli to my mom.

She cursed him, "I killed you once, I'll do it again."

Using her flying powers drawn from the air, she raised a hurricane to destroy the electric wire cage and freed herself and my dad.

Chapter 13

Feeling stressed out, Eli was thinking to himself. If I had a way to get Emily not to use her powers against me? There's got to be a way... oh yeah, I think there's a red gem that could take away her powers but I don't know about her daughter. I don't know if it will work on her too. I think it's called Element, like her hero name. If I got some, I could stop Emily from using her powers against me. She would be powerless to stop me.

Emma came up to him to ask him if she could do anything for him? He said, "No, it's okay. I was just thinking of a way to stop Emily from using her powers. I think I know a way to slow her down. There's a gem that Emily used when we fought 10 years ago. When her boyfriend, now husband, killed me."

"Are you sure I can't do anything to help you relax?"

"Well, you are a woman. Come with me. I want to show you the stars outside."

So, they went outside, and all of a sudden, he kissed her. She kissed him back and then the two went for a walk.

Eli and Emma were talking a walk by the lake in the moonlight. A full moon was present and the sky glowed from so many stars. They held each other's hand as they walked. They found an open area in the trees by the lake. Eli started kissing emma's neck, then he kissed her on the lips. She slowly starts to unbutton her shirt and unclasps her bra. Eli lays Emma down on a soft grassy patch and begins to slowly kiss her body, moving south. He licks and suckles on her beautiful breasts. She moans loudly, holding on to Eli. He licked, kissed and suckled on her breats as they shone in the moonlight for ten whole minutes.

Then he starts kissing her body, slowly inching lower. Eli pulls her pants down and takes her panties off. Eli begins licking Emma's pussy in long strokes. She moans louder and louder, whispering, "Yes, yes, more, more Eli". He makes sure to suckle on her now engorged clit, sliding his tongue deep inside Emma's now dripping wet pussy. Once Eli knew Emma was wet enough, he stops and lets her pull down his pants and boxers, revealing his long hard cock. She sucked on it furiously till it was dripping precum. He slowly got on top of Emma and started to rub her pussy with the tip of his dick to tease her and make her more wet for him. After enough teasing, he slowly inserted his dick into Emma's dripping wet vagina. He started off slow but as both of them get more into it, he starts going faster and faster, both moaning with pleasure. With Emma putting his arms around Eli, holding him close to her and telling him to fuck her faster with every thrust hitting her g-spot hard, it didn't take long before they were both at the brink. When they couldn't take it anymore, both of them arched each others backs, screaming loudly as they cummed together.

They collapsed in each other's arms in a passionate sweaty heap for a few minutes. They looked into each other's eyes and held each other close, covering each other in soft kisses as Eli kept his dick nuzzled inside Emma's pussy.

Chapter 14

Emma woke up in the morning in the bushes where they had slept with each other. She was feeling really sick, like she was pregnant or something. Is that even possible? Can the undead get pregnant? I shouldn't tell Eli just yet. I will say I'm sick with the flu or something. I don't want to add to his stress. All he thinks of is Emily and her daughter.

Emma was jealous that Eli was thinking about other girls and not her but why? Did Eli sleep with me to take some stress off or did he really want to? She was questioning her feelings about Eli. Did she really love Eli or was it just lust? She didn't know what it was.

But one way for sure, I have to be tested to see if I am pregnant or just sick. She went to a store and got a test done. She peed on the test and it was positive. She was thinking to her self, WHAT THE FUCK AM I GOING TO TELL ELI? THAT A BITCH LIKE ME IS PREGO! She was freaking out in the store bathroom! Okay, I need to tell Eli this. What would he say to me? He'd probably say, "Get rid of it bitch!" or something like that. Do I want to get rid of the baby? Zack would be a big brother and Eli would be a father. Wow! Eli, a dad!

She laughed. Yeah, he would not be the nicest dad any way. But I gotta tell him.

Chapter 15

She had the nerve to tell Eli about their baby but maybe after a few drinks, she thought to herself. How will she tell Eli about the baby? She went to the liquor store to get something for Eli to drink. She got rum, whiskey, and a bottle of vodka. She was at the cash register to buy them. Then she would tell Eli how she feels and about the baby.

She went home with the liquor in her hands. She came to Eli's office and offered him a drink.

"Do you want a drink, Eli?"

He assented, "I would love one."

She poured him a drink and another and another untill he was so drunk that she could say anything to him.

"ELI, I'M PREGNANT."

"Who's the father?"

She pointed at him and said, "You are the father, Eli." "But we didn't fuck." He thought to himself, wait, we did fuck in the bushes yesterday?

Emma yelled, "I LOVE YOU ELI. I have loved you for a long time now."

Eli said, "I feel the same," and kissed her stomach. "We have to raise it to be evil and it might inherit my powers."

Emma interjected, "Hey, it could get mine too!"

He leaned in to kiss her but was too drunk to try and passed out on her lap. As he was sleeping, she kissed him on the lips and whispered, "When you wake up, I'll tell you everything."

Chapter 16

Listening to their conversation on the communicator, Lilyanna couldn't believe that they were going to try to bring back a dragon that has been sealed for a thousand years. They are going to use my dear baby brother to do so. What does he have to do with anything? He is only 8 years old. How can I get him back to our family again? Aunt Rachel was right. I'm going to need help with this rescue mission or get a damn magic sword or something!

I called my parents to see if any of their friends' kids could help me out. On the communicator, I asked my parents if any of their friend's kids could help but they said No. All their friends' kids are normal and have no special skills or powers. I thanked my parents and hung up.

The only thing to do was to find a dragon killing sword. But where would I find it? I looked on the internet but found nothing. Maybe the library would have something but is there a library near Aunt Rachel's house? I wondered to myself. I asked Aunt Rachel about it. She said, "Yes, but it's in the town. You have to hide your powers. The towns people don't like people with powers. They think that people with powers are all witches. So, please hide that you have them."

I agreed. We went to the library desk and asked the lady who works there if they have any books or magic swords?

She asks, "Why would you need that?"

"I'm doing a school project and it's on magic swords." I smiled at the lady.

She said, "Okay, follow me."

We followed the lady and she picked out a book called Blaziken. I started reading the book but soon time was up and the library was closing. I asked the lady where I could buy this book? The lady smiled and said, "You can have it. No one uses that book, so you can have it. I was so thankful that I thanked the lady nearly ten times before I left.

Chapter 17

Todd set off on his journey to get to the frostwyrm's raise to resurrect the dragon Borea and finally take his revenge upon Emily and Francis. Soon, he would rule the world. He kept Jack handcuffed to him so he wouldn't try to get away. If Zack tried anything stupid, or to escape, Todd would kick Zack in the gut.

Soon after Emily and Francis' pet phoenix relayed a message to Emily and Francis, telling them what Todd was up to. They quickly packed what they needed and headed towards the frostwyrm's raise to cut Todd off and put a stop his evil plans.

Chapter 18

After reading the book, I learned that the sword won't come out unless the person wielding it has no evil in their hearts. The person also has to have powers or the sword won't work for the user.

I set off to find the sword and have an adventure with Rachel by my side. Soon, we caught up with Eli's army, Zack and Emma. I saw that Emma was pregnant. I thought to myself, oh my god! Emma is pregnant! With who's baby? Was the daddy Todd or Eli?

I had to get closer to them to spy on them. I needed to find out what they were up to. Suddenly, a man came up to us and said, "What are you doing?"

He was wearing Eli's army outfit. Was he a guard?

He introduced himself as Joshua Dupis. "Just call me Josh", he said. He was about 6 feet tall with blue eyes and blonde hair. He looked so dreamy, but saving Zack and getting the sword comes first. Maybe then I'd think about getting a boyfriend. Probably someone who thinks my powers are cool and loves me for me.

I asked him if he was going to tell Eli that we were here?

He replied, "Nah. This is not what I want to do with my life."

"What do you want to do with your life?"

"I want to be a chef. I want to make people happy with my food but this job was the only job that was hiring at the time, so I took it."

"Do you want out of this job?"

"Yeah, I do."

He smiled at me. I thought his smile could light up the world.

He said to me, "You're very pretty, now that I've got a good look at you."

I blushed and thanked him.

Rachel teased me, "Ooh someone's got a crush."

I whispered to her, "I don't know him. How can I like him? I think he's good looking. I think dad and him would get along great. That's all."

Josh asks me, "Are you single?"

"Yeah, I am single", I reply.

"Want to go on a date with me?"

"Maybe, after all this is over. I have to kill Todd and get that sword or I can't save my brother or the world. I need that sword. Do you think you can get it?"

"Yeah. If you say yes to the date, I'll help you out."

I had no choice but to say, "Fine, I'll go out with you but we have to save the world first and then my brother. Then, we will go out, okay?

He smiled and said, "Okay."

When I read the book of Blaziken, it said that the person who wields the sword must have no evil in their heart. The sword must have a past, right? So, I read the book again and it seems that the person owned the sword was a woman. A man had helped her defeat evil with powers or magic.

"Oh yeah, I have powers by the way."

Josh was shocked at first but then he was cool with it. He said, "It's okay. I thought you or your friend might."

"She's my aunt and the coolest one too, because she is a fucking ninja."

Chapter 19

I and Josh sneaked up to a camp where Todd was staying the night. He is quietly cooking food over a campfire but he has at least 4 goons to help protect him. Near his tent, there's a cage that holds my brother Zack. I and Josh sneak up to where Todd has the sword. A crony of Todd sneaks up on us. I use my power to despatch him. That alerts Todd and he attacks me and Josh. A fight ensues between I and Josh versus Todd.

I use my powers and cause some damage to Todd. He distracts me for a millisecond and hits me, knocking me against a tree. I was knocked unconscious for a few minutes from the blow. Zack remembers that I am his sister and he knows I have come to save him. He cries, "Sis, wake up, wake up, sis."

Josh retaliates and him and Todd start throwing heavy punches at each other. Both were trying to see who would fall first. Todd gets an uppercut to his gut but he bounces back and knocks Josh down for a second. He takes a few seconds to gloat about finally beating Josh and getting his revenge against me and my family.

Josh swiftly kicks Todd in the balls as hard as he can. Todd screams in agony. Josh then nails Todd with a bone-rattling uppercut right to his jaw, breaking it in 3 places. It knocks him out cold. He quickly runs over to me and helps me up. l run over to Zack's cage. He cries knowing his big sister is alright. Both of us use our powers to break the magic imbued lock on Zack's cage, releasing him. Then we grabbed the sword from Todd's tent and ran towards the frostwyrm's lair as fast as possible. After Todd got knocked out, the 3 other goons ran away scared shitless.

Chapter 20

Josh wanted to get to know me really bad but we need the sword first. I reach for the sword and pull as hard as I can but I can't do it. But why? The book said that I must have no evil in my heart. So, why couldn't I?

I said to Josh, "Hey, can I see the book for one sec?"

He said, "Sure."

I start reading it. It said that a boy and a girl with no evil shall pull out the sword. So, josh and I both join our hands together and pull the sword out. It worked. The sword came out but out with it came Borea. It started to attack us with Todd on his back. It was too late now. Borea was awake and very mad at us. We didn't know why.

I asked Borea, "Why are you so mad at us? We didn't do this to you."

But all he said was, "No, but your ancestors did. So, I will take my revenge. Your ancestors killed my wife and son and locked me in here for a thousand years."

He attacked us but Eil blocked it with his powers and saved Josh and me from being hit. I looked at him, very confused.

I asked him, "Why did you save us? You are with him, aren't you?"

Eli said, "Todd has gone mad with power. We need to stop him or kill him if it comes to that."

Todd jumped down from Borea's back as it was just going to attack us again. As he was going to blast us, he realized that it wasn't our fault it our asshole ancestors had done bad things. It wasn't us. The past is in the past.

By using his powers, it attacked Todd. Todd screamed and bellowed, "What are you doing? They are the bad guys, not me. They hurt you so bad and now you attack me?"

He turned to Eli, pleading to save him but Eli didn't help him at all. He screamed.

"I hope all of you go to hell." As he said that, Borea attacked him and killed him with one of his ice spears which were all around him.

But Borea said to us, "You need to kill me. I want to see my family again."

I said, "You saved us." I smiled and thanked him. I asked him, "Are you sure about this?

"Yes."

Borea cried so loudly that the earth shook. I took Borea's life. He looked up to me and said, "You look just like him right now." Borea started to shine like a star in the sun. With one cut to his heart, Borea was dead and I got Zack back. I hugged him so tight like I did not want to ever let go of him.

Chapter 21

We all started to walk back to the village. I had to set Todd's body on fire to make sure he stays dead and no one brings him back to life like Eli. The wind blew his ashes away. We had a funeral for Borea. We didn't set his body on fire. We used ice. With my ice powers, I covered his body with ice, since he was an ice dragon. That's when I saw a dragon egg near his body. His son was in the egg. I walked slowly towards the egg and examined it closely. It was still alive. I took the egg and started to warm it up. But I thought to myself, maybe it needs ice because Borea was an ice dragon. Maybe it should be cooled down. So, I cooled it down with my body, using my powers.

Every one looked at me funny. Josh said, "What is in your dress?"

I took the egg out and told him, "I found Borea's son. He's alive."

"I thought he died with his wife."

"Yeah, so did I, but it looks like he's very much alive and moving. I think he might hatch very soon."

"What are you going to name him?", asked Josh.

"I'll call him Pendrill."

Josh smiled. "It's a good name for him. We will tell him all about his dad and the things he did in his life. When we get back to your home, do you want to go on a picnic date?"

I smiled and joked with him, "I love that idea. You can show me how good a cook you are."

Now what should we do with Eli and Emma? We can't kill them. Eli saved me and Emma is pregnant. She looks like she's going to give birth soon.

All of a sudden, Emma started to yell. "My water broke!"

Eli carried her to the cave and asked her to marry him. She said yes.

I told him to get out. "I'll help her give birth."

She pushed as hard as she could and after 3 hours of labour, she gave birth to a baby boy. He was named Arthur James St. Peters.

"We are all done. Do you want to meet your son Eli?", I asked him. He went into the cave and saw his baby and the new mama. Rachel ripped some of her clothes off for the baby and it was wrapped in torn clothes.

Chapter 22

Josh and I were on a date to celebrate my 19th birthday. We were on a secluded private beach owned by my parents who were in town, shopping for the day. We ate appetizers of bruschetta with balsamic vinegar and parm cheese, a lobster bisque, a croque monsieur and jello for dessert.

We were lying on a blanket in the shade under a tree. I looked lovingly into Josh's baby blue eyes. He leaned in and gave me a passionate kiss on the lips. A slight moan drifted out of my lips. I whispered into his ears, "I want you...."

He started to kiss my neck and slowly undressed me. It wasn't long before my full breasts with their perky nipples were exposed to him for the first time. Josh started to massage my breasts with his hands. He continued to kiss me passionately on the lips and caressed my neck. Kissing along my slender neck, he starts to lick and caress my now erect nipples with his tongue. I moan a little louder. He plays with my breasts for 10 mins before he slowly starts to kiss a trail down my exposed belly. He plays and teases my belly button, making my moan and giggle.

Then he pulled down my bikini bottom, exposing my hairless virgin pussy to him for the very first time. I told Josh to please be careful, this is my first time. He rubs his finger up and down my clit in long strokes to get me wet. Then he slides his tongue deep into my pussy, tasting my wetness for the first time. He tells me it tastes amazing. He lapped up my pussy slowly but methodically until I started to arch my back and cummed hard. Josh had a wet face as I ejaculated all over him. He only smiled. I told him that it was my first orgasm that was not from my fingers or a toy.

Josh pulled down his bathing trunks, exposing a pretty good sized dick, not big not small but girthy. I gave him a condom to slide over his dick and told him to please take it slow. Josh nodded. He started to nuzzle his dick in between my legs and slowly broke through my hymen. We started to fuck for the first time.

As we got aroused further, Josh started to thrust faster and faster, hitting my g-spot. My moans got louder until I couldn't take it. I was about to scream and Josh was on the brink of ecstasy. We moaned together as both of us were hit by a massive orgasm.

The both of us collapsed in each other's arms, lying in a sweaty heap. We kissed and laid there for 5 mins, cuddling each other, with Josh's now almost limp dick still nuzzled inside of me. Lying spent after we were finished, we decided to go skinny dipping. The water was cool and refreshing.

Chapter 23

In a panic, Josh said, "The egg is hatching."

Josh and I got dressed and ran up to the village. We went inside the cold room where the egg was being kept. Zack came up to us and then ran up to my mom and dad.

I said, "How we going to going to get in the room?"

My mom said, "We are going to use our powers at the same time to get through the magic door."

I agreed to her idea. I used ice and she used water to open the magic door. We got in and I rushed over to see the egg. It had already hatched. I saw the cutest little dragon in its place. I started to cry when I saw it. I gave it some dragon milk which we got off the black market. It was hard to find but we did it. The baby dragon opened its eyes and its mouth, feeling very attached to me. I guess it thinks I'm his mother or something.

Then a strange old woman came to the village. Of course, our guards stopped her but she used her powers and froze them in place. She came up to me and Josh and said, "What a cute couple I see."

I said to her, "We aren't a couple yet. We had one date, that's it."

But she looked at my stomach and said, "You're pregnant with twins."

"Wait, I am what?"

I was in shock. Even my parents were shocked from the news but Josh was the most shocked. He wasn't mad. He simply got on one knee and asked me to marry him.

I asked him if he truly loves me? Then I'd marry him. But if he asked me to marry him just because I'm pregnant with his baby inside of me, then I won't do it.

"Lilyanna, I do love you. I have loved you since I met you. I think you are a very beautiful woman. Now you will have my kids. I'm going to always protect you and our babies."

My dad said to Josh, "If you are going to protect my daughter and my grandchildren, I'm going to let you train as a ninja. As Lilyanna's baby bump grows, she is going to need you more."

Josh agreed to become a ninja for Lillyanna's safely. He knew she won't be able to use her powers to protect herself since she is pregnant.

As soon as Josh agreed to become a ninja, my dad dragged him off to train. The moment Josh looked at me, I yelled, "Yes, I'll marry you."

I blushed as he smiled but didn't say anything. Zack, I, and my mom went to the nursery where my mom had given birth to Zack and me. My mom cried and said, "My little girl is pregnant and getting married."

Chapter 24

The old woman told us that there was a prophecy about my twins. A dragon will come to take revenge on your family for killing Borea. It's his sister. She is not like the other dragons. She also has a human form. Her name is Saavededar. Look out for her and her human form. In her human form, she has voodoo powers. In her dragon form, she has black ice powers and she can freeze any thing that comes in her way. She will come here and she will curse your family but not for another ten years.

I asked the old woman, "What do my kids have to do with her revenge? Doesn't she want revenge on me? I am the one that killed her brother but he wanted to die to see his wife and son again. But the thing is, his son is alive. He is just a baby right now. He can't do anything to help me if she wants revenge. It should be me and only me. Why does my family need to suffer when I'm the one that killed her only brother. I should be the one she curses."

Feeling sick to my stomach, I had to lie down after talking to the old woman. She left with out saying another word to us. I guess she did her job and warned us about Borea's sister coming to curse us. We need to get ready for what's to come.

Chapter 25

Some months passed and I gave birth to our twins. Josh and I were thinking of baby names for them. We named the girl Annabelle and the boy Jacob.

After the twins were born, Josh and I got ready for our wedding. My dad was his best man since he didn't have friends. My dad and my brother were on his side and my mom was my maid of honour. My aunt Rachel, and some of my mother's friends like Julia, Ben and Gray were also there. We said our vows and kissed. We were married.

But what's to come in our future ? What will we do about the prophecy? We have to find help soon, in case we are all fucked.

Chapter 26

Once the wedding was over, we had to decide whether to send Eli and Emma to jail or keep them here with their son Arthur. We must keep them on a tight leash. After what they had done, they should go to jail. But which one? I was thinking Bloodbane Maximum Security Prison for people with powers like they have.

I told everyone about it. My mom thought it was a good idea. Just us and their son will be able to visit them. So, we sent Eli and Emma to jail where they can no longer hurt anyone or themselves. Of course, they will be separated but I think they should be married. They aren't going to see each other for a long time. We have to talk to them about it.

Chapter 27

My parents talked to Emma and Eli about the situation they are in right now. My mom told them to get married now and go to jail in the morning. Or they would be on a very short leash and becomes our slaves forever.

"But you will have some freedom after your duties. Arthur will not be a slave to us. Instead, he will be taken in by our daughter Lillyanna and her husband Josh. The choice is up to you. If you choose to be our slave, you will have to wear a leash. You can never go against us or the twins. What do you pick?"

Eli said, "We have to think about it. Can we?"

My dad said "Yes, of course you can. I mean, I hate you Eli but my wife thinks you have some good in you but I think you are still evil. So is your fiancé. But you did help get my son back which I don't understand. Why did you do that? You're still a dick though. I'll find a way to kill you again with your soon-to-be wife, even if you're Zombies now, if you try to kill Emily or our daughter and our grandchildren.

Eli laughed. "Don't worry. I don't want to kill Emily anymore because I have my own family to take care of. I am going to jail for my crimes. I pick jail over being your slave. Being your slave is creepy. I hate you too. You're a dick too and you did kill me with a bloody rock over and over again."

My dad laughed, "Yup, I'll do it all over again."

My dad talked to my mom and told her that Eli had picked jail. "He hates me because I killed him with a rock in the past. He thinks I am a dick too."

"What did Emma say?"

"Yeah. She also picked jail. So, we have to marry them and then send them to Bloodbane Maximum Security Prison for people with powers in the morning."

We set up the wedding and Eli and Emma said their vows. They kissed and then, they were married. They spent the night with their son. In the morning, they were separated. Eli went to the men's wing and Emma went to the woman wing.

"That's the end of them," my parents said, but my mom was crying a little bit. She knew Eli and Emma had some good in them but it was for the best.

Chapter 28

(Ten years later.)

The twins are now ten years old and Arthur is 11 years old. He still visits his parents who are in jail. The twins promise to get them out of prison someday. Everyone was old and falling asleep but the young children. The kids saw a woman standing there, then she was gone. Who would have done this?

The End...

To be continued... find out who has done this to the grown ups.